For my dog Polly Pocket,
who knows a lot about poop, and is the ultimate gift.
—S. B.

For Biff and HoneyBun,
who encouraged my artistic pursuits.
—M. G.

Henry Holt and Company, *Publishers since 1866*
Henry Holt® is a registered trademark of Macmillan Publishing Group, LLC
120 Broadway, New York, NY 10271 • mackids.com

Library of Congress Cataloging-in-Publication Data is available.

Our books may be purchased in bulk for promotional, educational, or business use.
Please contact your local bookseller or the Macmillan Corporate and Premium Sales Department at
(800) 221-7945 ext. 5442 or by email at MacmillanSpecialMarkets@macmillan.com.

First edition, 2022
The illustrations in this book were created using Adobe Photoshop CS3;
real mixed media, including pencil, paper, and acrylic; and a mercurial Wacom Cintiq.
Printed in China by RR Donnelley Asia Printing Solutions Ltd., Dongguan City, Guangdong Province

ISBN 978-1-250-83710-3 (hardcover)
1 3 5 7 9 10 8 6 4 2

THE VERY MERRY POOP CHRISTMAS

written by

Samantha "Bergerbuns" Berger

illustrated by

Manny "On-the-Canny" Galán

Henry "Don't-Holt-it-in" Holt and Company

New York

SANTA, PLEASE BRING...

♥ Penny

Poop had never been so popular in the world (or "poopular," as the case may be), and every kid had poop-ified wishes on their Christmas wish lists.

When the North Pole caught a whiff of this news . . .
everyone gasped, "HUH? Whaaa? Eww!"

But then, slowly, they started to get excited.

But a certain someone (whose name started with an "S" and ended in an "—anta Claus") just couldn't jump on the poop bandwagon.

He didn't care for poop humor. Especially at Christmas.

Mrs. C knew Santa could be stubborn.
But then again, so could she.

And she wanted a very poopy
Christmas, just as much as kids did.

She thought maybe if she decorated, and pooped the place up, it might change Santa's mind.

So Mrs. Claus and all the elves lit up Christmas Village with winky-stinky poo lights.

They trimmed the trees in dingle-bells and sparkly poo-balls.

They hung a potty-seat
wreath on every door.

But Santa wasn't saying, **Ho-Ho-Ho**.
Santa was saying, **No-No-No**.

"I just don't think Christmas is the time for poop,"
said Santa. "Christmas is a time for peace."

Mrs. Claus knew Christmas was a time for peace,
but she wondered if it could also be a time for poop.

Inside, they put a poop Yule log in the
fireplace, and a golden plunger atop the tree.

They hung up undies
on the mantel with care.

They baked
gingerbread
OUThouses!

But Santa didn't say, **Feliz Navidad**. Santa said, **Feliz NaviDON'T**.
"I just don't think Christmas is the time for poop," said Santa.
"Christmas is a time for love."

The elves knew Christmas was a time for love,
but they wondered if it could also be a time for poop.

In the workshop, the elves got to work inventing very poopy toys like–

A Doggo-Makes-a-Loggo!

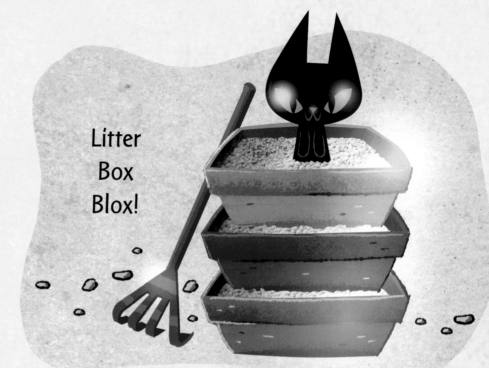

Litter
Box
Blox!

And dump trucks that truck dumps!

"Christmas is a time for joy. Peace, love, joy,
and goodwill toward every living being. I'm afraid
there will NOT be poop at Christmas," said Santa firmly.

"And that's my final word."

tee hee...

tee hee tee hee heh hee

ha ha ha ha ha ha

Ho! Ho! Ho! Ho!

"Ahhh, I get it now!" said Santa.
"Christmas is a time for peace, joy, and love. But it's also a time for **laughter**!
I think maybe we could have a very poopy Christmas, after all!"
"Yaaaaay!" everyone cheered.

The reindeer were so joyous, they high-hooved and played new poo-pendous reindeer games like —

The Gotta-Go Limbo!

Leap to the Loo!

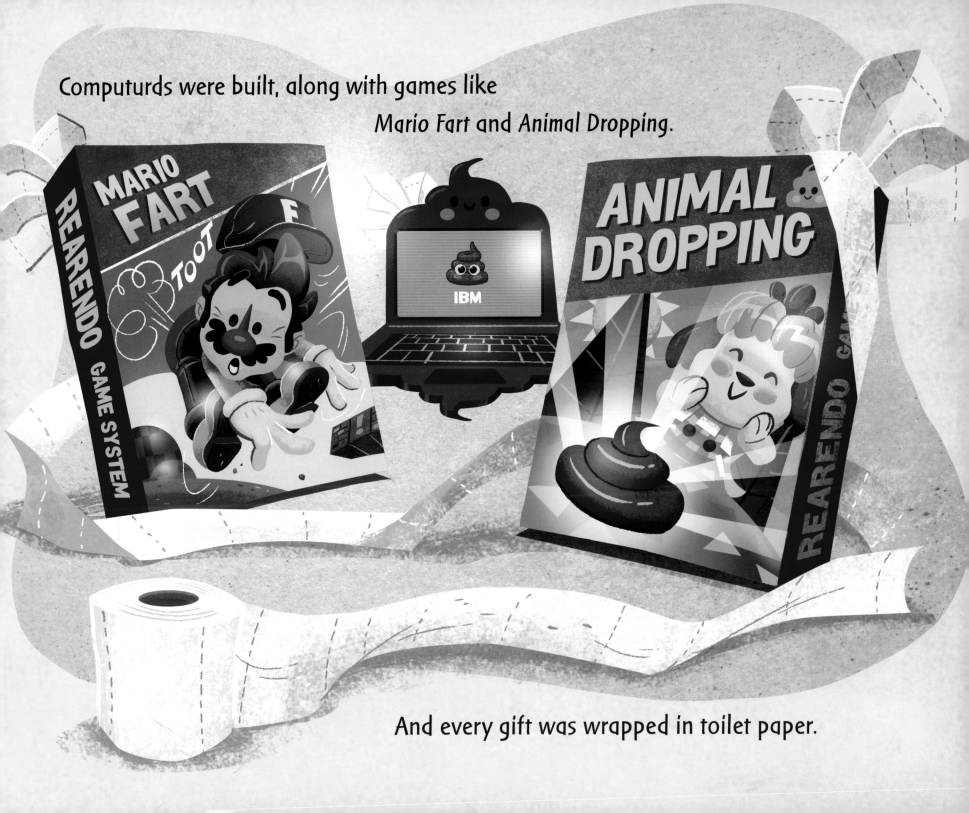

Computurds were built, along with games like

Mario Fart and Animal Dropping.

MARIO FART

TOOT

REARENDO GAME SYSTEM

IBM

ANIMAL DROPPING

REARENDO GAME SYSTEM

And every gift was wrapped in toilet paper.

But Santa didn't say, 'Tis the season.
Santa said, 'Tis NOT the season.
"I truly don't think Christmas is
the time for poop," said Santa.

And The Buttcracker Suite.

Then everyone put on their ugliest Christmas poop sweaters, gathered round the piano, and caroled songs like . . .

"Jingle Smells,"

"I'm Dreaming of a Brown Christmas,"

and "Silent (But Deadly) Night."

Everybody in the North Pole was laughing!

(Santa, most of all!)

They loaded up Santa's sleigh with all the poopy presents and blasted off!

They were so in the Christmas spirit that Poodolph the Brown-Nosed Reindeer lit up the sky with a big poop emoji for all the world to see.

That Christmas Eve, not only did Santa come down the chimney, fill stockings, and leave presents . . .

he also built snowmen—
pooping pebbles!
And he TP'd the trees!

He left little packages of
reindeer-dropping treats for everyone!
And a very special card, saying . . .

PEACE, LOVE, JOY . . .
AND LAUGHTER
TO ALL!

Santa!

From the Kitchen of Mrs. Claus:

RECIPE FOR

"REINDEER DROPPING TREATS"

Ingredients

- 1 cup chocolate chips
- ½ cup creamy peanut butter
- 6 cups corn pop cereal
- ½ cup cocoa powder
- 1½ cups powdered sugar

Santa's Favorite!

Directions:

1. Dump the chocolate chips and peanut butter into a microwave-safe bowl, and microwave for 30 seconds at a time, stirring in between, until melted.

2. Plop ALL the corn pop (or corn *poop*) cereal into the warm goo, and mix to coat.

3. Scoop the cocoa powder and powdered sugar into a large sealable plastic bag, drop in the corn pop glop, and SHAKE-A SHAKE-A SHAKE-A till it's all coated.

4. Let it cool on a tray and serve it up! Fresh reindeer droppings for all!

So easy!   Ten minutes!   Not real poop!